A Mathematical Story about Saving and Growing Money

COMPOUND INTEREST

Illustrated by Erin Davey-Jepson

Abbas Kazerooni

RED PANDA

Published by Red Panda, an imprint of Westland Books, a division of Nasadiya Technologies Private Limited, in 2024

No. 269/2B, First Floor, 'Irai Arul', Vimalraj Street, Nethaji Nagar, Alapakkam Main Road, Maduravoyal, Chennai 600095

Westland, the Westland logo, Red Panda and the Red Panda logo are the trademarks of Nasadiya Technologies Private Limited, or its affiliates.

ISBN: 9789360459413

10 9 8 7 6 5 4 3 2 1

This is a work of fiction. Names, characters, organisations, places, events and incidents are either products of the author's imagination or used fictitiously.

Printed at Nutech Print Services, India

The **squirrel** and the **ferret**, a cousin of the mole, lived on farms next to each other. They were new farmers and excited to grow their **first crop** with **a corn kernel** each.

They **sowed** the corn kernel. **Watered** and **fed** their corn. And waited for them to grow.

Soon the kernels started **growing**. They watched the ears form and were amazed to see them take shape.

They were excited about the **harvest.**

On harvest day, the squirrel and the ferret ran to their fields, waving like friendly neighbours. Now, each of them had **one stalk with five corn cobs** each.

'I'm going to pick all the corn and save it for **winter,**' said the squirrel. 'We'll be hungry, and this will feed my family.'

'Oh, that's smart,' the ferret replied.
'But I have other plans,' he continued.

The squirrel was curious about what the ferret was doing in his field next door.

'I'll **save** most of my corn too,' the ferret added, 'but not all.'

'Will you eat some of it now?' asked the squirrel.

'Oh no, no,' the ferret shook his head. **'I won't touch my precious corn until winter.** I'll eat what I find in the forest and field till then.'

'So, if you're not saving all the corn and not eating what's left over, what will you do with the rest?' the squirrel was confused.

The ferret smiled. 'Dear squirrel, I like to **save**, just like you. But I save to make more from what I started with (which is called interest). This is called **compound interest**.'

'Wow!' The squirrel gasped. 'You're so clever, ferret. But I'm still confused. What is compound interest?'

'I can show you, **friend**,' the ferret said.

The squirrel, eager to hide his corn for winter, said impatiently, 'Not now, Ferret. Maybe later?'

'Whenever you wish,' the ferret smiled and went on his way.

The squirrel picked all his corn and **hid** it in a **secret** place, so that he could eat it in the **cold months** of winter.

On the other hand, the ferret saved **four corn for winter** and the remaining **one corn for planting** the next year. The squirrel watched the ferret work in the fields, puzzled.

Winter came and the squirrel ate and ate and stuffed his belly with the corn he had grown, **leaving only one kernel, to plant** a stalk again. He felt smug and happy, thinking he had more than his neighbour.

The ferret also ate well, but he didn't touch the two corns he had kept aside. He knew that **today's small loss means tomorrow's profit.**

Summer came and the squirrel was ready to plant his single **kernel of corn** for another harvest. He looked across the fence and to his surprise, he saw there were **five stalks of corn** growing on the ferret's side.

'How did you do that?' the squirrel asked.

'I wanted to tell you, but you were in a rush,' the ferret replied. 'Do you remember how I put one whole corn away, at harvest time? In spring, **I planted the extra kernels** and now I have five stalks of corn!'

The squirrel was **amazed**.
Surely this was luck.

The squirrel had just being following the way his daddy saved and before him his granddaddy, year after year. He was scared of trying something new.

It was harvest time once again. The squirrel watched the ferret **save three stalks of corn** for the **winter** and **stashed away two stalks of corn to** plant in **spring**.

The ferret worked harder this year.
And he did it with a smile, singing his
favourite **song**:

Interest, interest, compound interest;
My favourite type of interest is compound interest.
I plough, I till, I pound,
Working to create more interest each year.
I keep adding the interest to make more.
Interest, interest, compound interest.
My favourite type of interest is **compound interest**.

'Don't be sad, squirrel,' said the ferret. 'I'll help you do the same.'

'Really?' asked the squirrel excited.

'Of course,' replied the ferret. 'With **hard work and patience**, we'll **fill our fields** in less than five years.'

'That's amazing,' said the squirrel. 'Thank you.'

'You are welcome,' said the ferret. **'The bigger the risk, the bigger the gain.'**

Every year, the two friends worked hard in their fields singing:

Interest, interest, compound interest;
My favourite type of interest is compound interest.
I plough, I till, I pound,
Working to create more interest each year.
I keep adding the interest to make more,
Interest, interest, compound interest.
My favourite type of interest is compound interest.

In five years, ferret and squirrel both had **fields full of corn.** The squirrel thanked the ferret, knowing he would still have only one stalk of corn, each year, if he hadn't learned about compound interest.

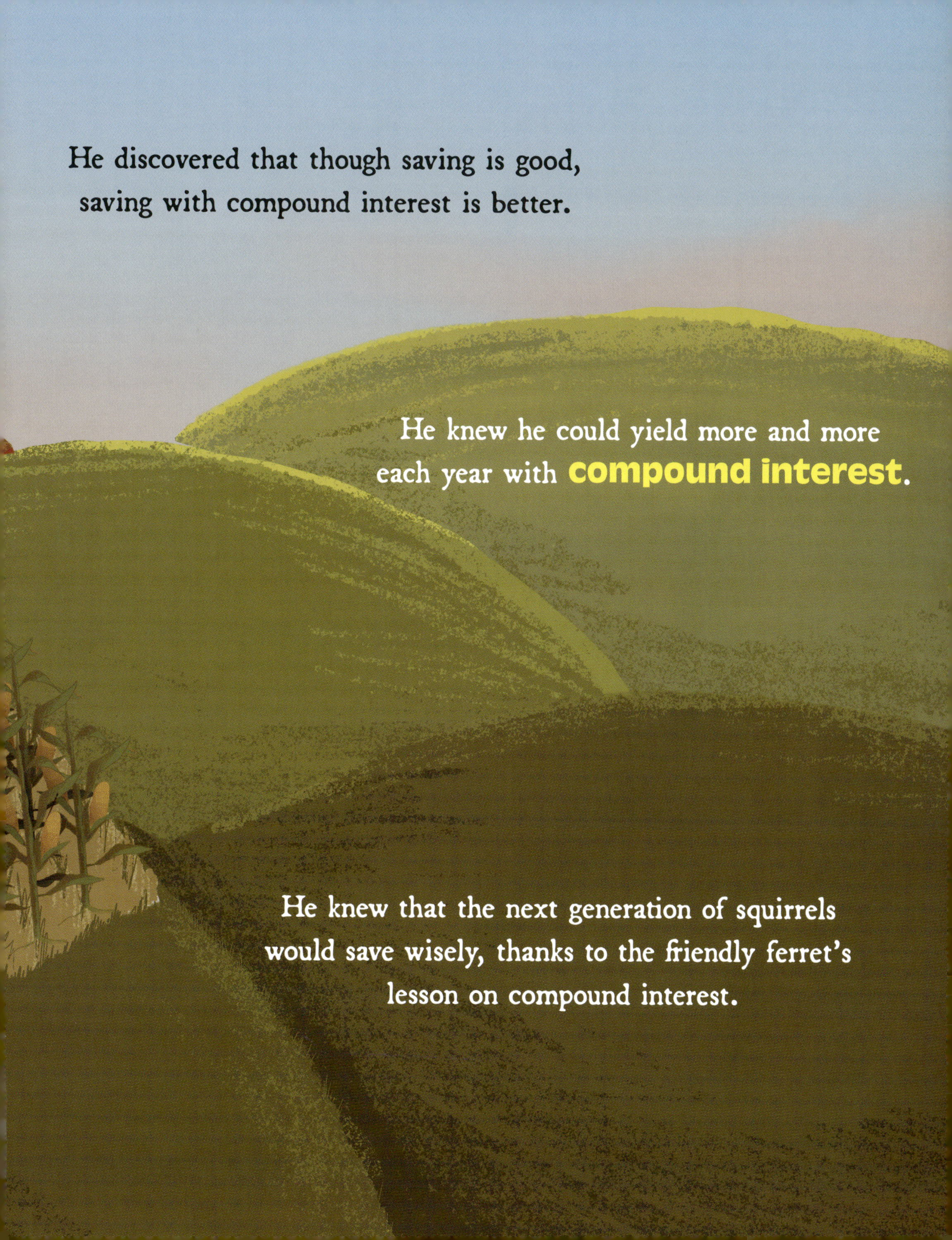

He discovered that though saving is good, saving with compound interest is better.

He knew he could yield more and more each year with **compound interest**.

He knew that the next generation of squirrels would save wisely, thanks to the friendly ferret's lesson on compound interest.

Understanding Compound Interest

- Isn't it cool how both the squirrel and ferret started with just one corn kernel. Their harvest was the same—five corn cobs on a stalk.

- Both the friends were cool and saved food for winter but the ferret saved some for the next season too. This is like saving money—you spend some and put some aside for later use.

- However, the ferret also used a special trick called compound interest. By planting extra corn each year, he grew more stalks and got more corn. Over time, his harvest grew much bigger. This is like earning interest (additional money) on saved money, and here you make more money on the interest (additional money) you've already earned.

- The squirrel learned that while saving is important, using compounc interest makes savings grow faster. Are you like the ferret too?

- So now, do you realise that compound interest helps money grow more each year? And that if you keep saving wisely you can make your money grow wisely too

How to Make Your Money Grow

Just like the ferret, do you know you can also save your money and make it grow using compound interest. Here's the trick, if you have ₹100:

1. Save: If you put your ₹100 in a special place, like a piggy bank, the money will be safe for a rainy day. But, it will always be ₹100. This is like planting a corn kernel.

2. Save Wisely: But if you put your ₹100 in a bank, your money will grow.

3. Earning Interest: When you save money in a bank, the bank pays you some more money called interest. Let's say the bank gives you 10 per cent interest every year. So, after one year, your ₹100 becomes ₹110.

4. Reinvest Your Interest: Now, if you invest and don't spend that extra ₹10 or your original ₹100, like the ferret, you will earn interest on ₹110, not just ₹100.

5. Watch it Grow: Every year, your earning investment and earning will both be bigger. After the second year, your ₹110 becomes ₹121. After the third year, it grows to ₹133.10, and so on.

6. Be Patient: If you are patient like the ferret with your money, the longer you keep it saved, the more it will grow.

By saving your money and letting the compound interest build up over time, your ₹100 can almost be double in nearly seven years, just like ferret's corn!

Abbas Kazerooni, also known as Abbas Kazerounian, is the acclaimed author of two internationally best-selling novels, *On Two Feet and Wings* and *The Boy With Two Lives*. In addition to his writing career, Abbas is a multifaceted professional working as a lawyer, professor of law and actor in the United States. He is a founding partner of Kazerouni Law Group, APC, specialising in consumer rights and class actions, where he represents individuals against Fortune 500 companies. Outside of his professional life, Abbas enjoys travelling to rare destinations, sampling global cuisine and wine, working out and playing tennis.

The red panda is a reddish-brown mammal with a long, ringed tail and a raccoon-like face. Also called a firefox, it is found in the forest of the eastern Himalayas. In India, it lives in Sikkim, Arunachal Pradesh, in the Darjeeling district of West Bengal, and parts of Meghalaya. Its diet includes bamboo shoots and leaves, grass, fruit, roots and insects. The cat-sized red panda uses its bushy tail for balance and to wrap around its body for warmth up in the mountains.The red panda is now an endangered species, with less than 10,000 left in the wild.